Storm Birds

David G Evans

Table of Contents

Varujan was on vacation in Barcelona Spain, he'd been working for a year before he was able to go on vacation. His fiancé was in Connecticut visiting with her family, who she hadn't seen in two months.

An alert came over his phone saying that Texas was hit by an asteroid. In an hour, he would be leaving to go to the rodeo. He's been going to rodeos since he was 13 years old. His nephew used to ride bulls for a living,

But his health didn't hold up for very long, and he had to quit riding bulls. He got tired of sitting and waiting in the hotel room and went out for a walk down the sidewalk. He came to a small coffee shop called Bevendo and stepped inside.

Sitting at one of the tables was a man with a blue mohawk, sipping on his coffee. A mother of two sat in the back corner, the one kid was eating a piece of donut that his mother had given to him.

While the other kid was smiling and taking in the sights. Varujan was reading the coffee menu, there were types of coffee that he never heard of.

"Are you ready to order Sir?"

"No," I'm just looking over the different types of coffee.

Just tell me when you're ready to order, I'll do that. A man with a rough looking face walked in with his dog that was on a leash. Varujan kept an eye on the man, his presence made him feel uncomfortable.

The mother of two finished up drinking her coffee and quickly exited the place. The man walked over to the counter, and said I'd like a cup of black coffee with no sugar in it.

The man's dog wasn't very sociable and it just laid down by his feet. Varujan wanted to bend down and pet the dog, but something in his mind told him not to. After a few minutes the man behind the counter handed the man his cup of coffee.

Varujan took notice to the holster on the man’s belt and distanced himself away from the man further. Surprisingly the man’s dog got up, and brought it’s paw up onto the counter. This brought a smile to the people standing behind the counter, then the dog got down from the counter.

When Varujan saw the man put his hands by his waist he got uncomfortable. He was hoping that the man was going to leave soon. After paying for his coffee, the man turned around and walked out of the place.

“Do any one of you know that man personally?”

“No,” but he makes us feel very uncomfortable every time he comes here.

Before we worked here there was a terrible shooting at this coffee shop, and several people lost their lives.

We used to have two televisions in here on all of the time, but the customers began to complain that the news was offending them.

So, the next day the manager came in and took out all the televisions. I'm ready to order, I'd like an espresso, coming right up. He handed the man the money and peered out the window.

A man walked past with a cast on his arm, a few minutes after that, he saw bulls running past the coffee shop. He couldn't believe what he was seeing.

"Are you fellas seeing this?"

"Yes," it's unbelievable.

2 police officers entered the shop, with stern looks on their faces. One of them spoke up saying this area is currently under a state of emergency. A woman sitting at the table near the window was flabbergasted after hearing the news.

Excuse me officer said the woman, but if I don't get out of here soon, I'll be late to the charitable event. We're not saying that you have to stay in this shop, you can leave at any time at your own discretion.

The woman threw away her coffee, then headed out. Varujan was now sitting down comfortably at the table and drank the last sip of his coffee.

Both officers looked over at him, one of the officers walked over to him. I'd like to know how the bulls escaped the arena; it was because of ignorance.

> "How many bulls do you think are in that arena?"

> "A whole lot."

The bulls escaped from both arenas, and the staff that worked in both places ran for their lives. I'm just glad to see that the bulls left the streets, but that doesn't mean that people still aren't in immediate danger out there.

> "What if someone kills the bulls?"

> "Then they'll be sentenced for a long time in prison."

Chapter 1

One of the officers phone went off, he quickly picked it up. I’m talking to the chief of police and you and I have to go out on a special mission, come on let’s go.

Both officers rushed out of the shop and walked down the street to their vehicle. I put my key in the door to unlock it and it still won't open.

> “Are you playing some kind of trick on me?”
>
> “No,” I'm not.

Two angry bulls came up from behind them, then the officer turned around and saw them.

Both officers climbed up on top of the car to escape the bulls, the one bull came forward and rammed into the car.

Causing the officers to lose their balance, one of them fell off but quickly got back up on the car. Then the second bull came around to the other side of the car; one of us must lure them out of here.

If you do that you're definitely going to get gored, you're not going to stay here all day just because you're afraid to make a move.

The bulls horn hit one of the windows shattering it, you’re just allowing the bull to destroy our car. Yell at the bull or throw something at it.

I don't have anything to throw at it and yelling won't do anything. The braver officer got down from the car and quickly ran down the street, with the bulls following him.

They were catching up to him, he saw someone opening their door and ran inside, and bumped into one of the people inside.

> "What's going on with you officer asked a disgruntled man?"

> "I was being chased by two bulls down the street."

I didn't mean to disrespect any of you, then one of the bulls slammed into the door. At any movement that bull is going to break through the door, and pumble all of us.

Everyone in the room went up the steps to the second floor to hide out there from the bull. While this was happening, the other officer was still sitting on top of his car fearing for his life.

Suddenly a giant drone came flying towards him, when it was hovering just above him, he jumped up and grabbed onto it.

Amazingly it handled his weight and flew away above the rooftops. The higher it went the harder he held on to it.

While he was flying through the air, several short-toed eagles gave chase after him. The drone did some outlandish maneuvers around buildings, to try to lose the birds.

Eventually the birds stopped chasing after the drone, his phone was ringing but there was no way that he could answer it at the moment.

The drone dropped down closer to the ground, making him feel more at ease. The drone flew through someone's yard and crashed into a clothesline.

Causing the drone and the officer to fall to the ground with a thud. He saw a man wearing all black standing by his house.

> "What do you think you're doing in my neighbor's yard?"
>
> "The drone I was on crashed here."

As the officer was getting his bearings, the man pulled out a knife and walked towards him.

The policeman got into a fighting stance; the man tried forcing the knife into the officers chest. The officer made a last-ditch effort to stop the man, and stomped on his foot, and twisted his wrist until he dropped the knife.

Then the man gave the officer his shoulder in hopes that he could knock him to the ground. But this didn't faze the officer, and he tackled the man to the ground.

If you don’t stop fighting with me things are only going to get worse for you. The man attempted to reach for his knife, and the officer pushed it away from him. The officer forced the man's hands behind his back and took out his handcuffs and handcuffed him.

He could hear the sound of squealing tires, then not a minute later a black SUV showed up. Two men wearing black suits got out and shot tasers at the both of them.

Hitting the man and barely missing the officer, the officer ran to take cover behind a bush. The men in black just kept coming towards him, he immediately pulled his gun out of his holster.

When the men saw the gun they took cover too, and they said you won't be walking out of here alive officer.

Then the officer replied I bet that I do get out of here alive. The officer fired hitting one of the men, while they were shooting at him.

The man fell to the ground, while the other man found a different place to hide. The man fired and the bullet grazed the officers leg, then he fired back at the man hitting him in the chest causing him to collapse.

The driver of the SUV got out to stretch his legs and happened to see the bodies of the agents that he drove there. You shouldn't be over here Sir; this is an active crime scene.

"Do you have any weapons on you?"

"No."

"Who sent you out here to attack me?"

"I'm not going to disclose that to you."

I could arrest you for disrupting a crime scene, the man looked bewildered. I can see you looking at that body over there, you better not take anything from the dead man. The man backed away from the body, and five Falcons came flying over towards him.

He picked a rock and threw it at them, get out of here you dumb birds. As he was walking back to his truck, a massive bird came swooping down directly towards him and grabbed him by his shoulders and flew away with him.

The giant bird came from a testing facility, one of the 7 tests went awry. The bird grew from the size of a Sparrow to the size of a tetradactyl, before they're very eyes.

The scared lab workers immediately called for security, and the security man showed up. Just looking at the bird caused him to faint.

One of the brave lab workers dragged the unconscious man out of the way of the bird. The bird flapped its wings and knocked viles off tables and books.

Then it went after, the unconscious man's body. Pecking it and ripping it apart with its razor-sharp talons. It tried pecking one of the workers, but they threw the trash can at it, hitting it in the head.

This only angered the bird and it began trying to break through the glass window, it pecked the window several times and eventually it shattered and it flew out the window, escaping out into the city. The giant bird flew away with the man, this was a big relief for the officer. He pulled out his phone and called the other officer.

"Hello, where are you?"

"I'm at the station."

"What about you?"

"I don't even know where I am."

A large drone had flown over me, I grabbed onto it and it flew away with me. While I was flying I was attacked by some Eagles, after that the drone crashed into a clothesline.

"Where you hurt at all?"

"No," but I almost got shot.

"Who was shooting at you?"

"Men in suits who pulled up in a truck."

"What's your plan now?"

"To call a taxi and get back to the station."

"Where did you tell the chief I was at?"

"I told him that you got lost somewhere."

"What did he say to that?"

He said there's no time to be lost. I thought he would have said that he was very worried about me. He's in a very serious mood today, so don't set him off in any way or you'll get your walking papers.

"What happened to that bull that was chasing you down the street?"

"I ran inside someone's house to hide from it."

The people that lived there weren't so happy with me after I ran through their living room. Then the bull began slamming against the door and that's when all of us retreated upstairs.

Eventually the bull broke through the door and began smashing everything in the living room. I promised them I would give them some money to buy what got ruined. They said I was a very gracious man, I probably stayed with them for at least an hour.

I didn't have much of a walk back to the car, but I was always looking over my shoulder for a bull. When I finally got back in the car I drove down the street 1/4 while, and that's where the bulls were gathered together alongside the road.

One of them did come after me, but I was able to outmaneuver it, and continued down the road. I got to the station as quickly as I could, I was awfully lucky because I got there a few minutes before the chief did.

When he got there I was settled at my desk already working, he was glad to see me working. About 20 minutes later he came into my room and asked me about you, that's when I told him.

Thanks for letting me know all of this, you're welcome. I'll be at the station shortly; I'll talk to you then bye.

45 minutes later he arrived at the station, and he and the other officer and the chief had a long talk in the conference room.

Chapter 2

Varujan had left the coffee shop and went to the small sandwich shop on the corner. He ordered himself a Turkey club sandwich and a bowl of tomato bisque soup.

He took several bites out of his sandwich, then his fiancee gave him a call. She mentioned to him how much she missed him, and that she couldn't wait to be together again with him.

They continued the conversation for almost half an hour, then hung up with one another. He paid for his food, then he walked out of there and walked back to his hotel room. His phone began ringing and he picked it up.

Hello, this is space mission command, and I'm letting you know that we lost one of our space pilots a few hours ago.

He died because the rocket crashed into an asteroid, the humanoid robot took over the rest of the mission. We sent up a rescue drone to rescue him and rescued him just fine.

Your crew of specially trained astronauts are on their way up there to put together the new laser weapon. That's all the news that I have for you right now, if anything else changes just let me know, okay bye now.

Meanwhile the rocket that carried the first part of the laser weapon collided with an asteroid and violently crashed onto the planet Sepfium.

The human pilot was killed in the impact with the asteroid, but the space robot survived. Suddenly the robot came to life, and immediately went over to the human to see what he could do for him.

The robot saw blood dripping down the side of the humans space suit, it took the man out of his space suit so he could get a better look at his injuries.

His arm was broken in two places and had a broken neck. The robot picked up the man and took him outside of the craft and placed him on the ground. The robot knew that there was an emergency shovel somewhere inside of the craft.

He searched around the different compartments and soon came upon it. He unfolded the shovel and went over next to the man and began digging into the hard soil.

He dug down a few feet into the ground, then picked up the man and put him into the hole. The robot picked up the shovel and filled the hole with the dirt.

The robot looked up and saw that there was a dust storm coming its way, he quickly retreated back into the craft and locked everything up. Dust completely filled up the sky and everywhere else. The robot patiently waited for the dust storm to be over, a call came into the space phone.

The robot quickly picked it up, hello this is Droid 1 answering the phone.

“Can you put the human pilot on the phone?”

“No,” he's dead.

I can't hear you very well there seems to be an interference, it's because I'm in the middle of a dust storm.

“Are you still on your way to Lorphinetta?”

“No,” we have crashed, after colliding with an asteroid.

The craft is in critical condition, and fuel has leaked out of it.

“Have you made any repairs on the craft?”

“No,” it's too damaged.

The repair kit flew out of the craft when it collided with the asteroid.

“What kind of shape are the two propulsion engines in?”

“They're in bad shape one of the housings to the propulsion engines has cracked.”

“Are you standing in front of them right now?”

"No," outside there's a bad dust storm going on.

"Do you think you'll be able to get them to start up again?"

"No."

"Do you know where the black box is for the craft?"

"Yes."

"What kind of shape is that in?"

"It's in good shape."

In three hours, we're going to send up a team of astronauts along with three rockets with the laser weapon components to planet Lorphinetta. We're sending up a rescue drone up to you once it gets up there fly it over to planet Lorphinetta. Let me know once it gets up there.

"Did you see any life forms on the planet you're currently on?"

"No," I haven't.

"Would you like me to take any soil samples from this planet?"

"No."

"What's that beeping sound that I'm hearing?"

It's warning me that the pressure inside the cabin is building up too high, and the craft may blow up.

The dust storm was still going on, but the robot had no other choice and got out of the craft and took the phone with him.

“Hello, are you still there?”

“Yes,” I just exited the craft.

The craft exploded throwing the robot into the air, it fell to the ground on its side. The robot got up and saw that the space phone was missing, he reached down, and couldn't find it.

The ground all around him was covered in dust, he took a few steps and bent down searching through the dust, eventually he was able to find it.

He could hear Mission Control speaking through the phone. The rescue drone braved the dust storm and landed on the planet, near where the robot was standing.

The rescue drone just got here, good now be careful out there call me back if anything else goes awry, bye now.

The robot walked over to the drone and it opened up allowing him inside. He strapped himself in and programmed the drones GPS system to take him to planet Lorphinetta. After finishing up with the GPS, the drone took off into the sky.

On its way to its destination, it passed by 2 planets and went through several debris fields. It almost collided with 2 alien spaceships, and shot a warning shot out of the space canon at a robotic flying craft that got too close to it.

The drone passed by a destroyed outpost; missiles were fired out of the outpost but the drone quickly outmaneuvered them. A few minutes later the drone landed on planet Lorphinetta.

The robot exited the drone and walked over to the astronaut housing unit and typed in the code to open the door.

The door opened and the robot entered, it walked down a hall and entered a room off to the left. This was a robot rest room, he looked down at the power indicator on his arm.

It showed that he was at 75%. He pulled the charge cord out of the wall and plugged himself in and sat down on the chair.

He placed the space phone on the desk next to him, he opened one of the desk drawers and took out a small container full of oil.

He opened the container and poured some oil into the piston of his right arm. He figured that it would take a while for the team of astronauts and the rockets to get to the planet, so he closed his eyes and rested for a while.

Chapter 3

On Venus there was a lot of activity going on among the alien creatures, there are 4 different kinds of creatures that live on Venus.

Above the planet there are large frozen clouds, inside the clouds is a sinister creature that must not be woken at any cost.

It's a species of rare bird called a storm bird, when disrupted they become very aggressive lashing out at everything in their way, they can live for 592 years. Their bodies mysteriously become electrified, only when there flying.

Their beaks are long and sharp at the end, the birds had become frozen during the deep freeze period 35 years ago.

Much is known about its daily behaviors, the birds lived in the clouds and sometimes landed on the tops of trees.

Every time a thunderstorm occurs, the birds would wake up and aggressively go after the creatures below pecking and stabbing them with their sharp beaks, until the creatures left the area.

Then the birds will go back up in the clouds and settle down. The poolinta is a creature as small as a rabbit, with no tail. It's able to run at speeds of 60 mph and is able to breathe under the water.

This creature doesn't like to be bothered by the other creatures on the planet, it oftentimes digs a hole in the ground and hides in there for several hours. The next creature Xortinoomis is the size of a deer, it's an omnivore. It's lifespan is 10 years. This creature has muscular wings that allow it to fly for long distances, before having to take a rest.

This creature is much more social than the others are and intermingles with the other species. This creature likes to feed on the hopta plant, that has a sweet taste to it.

Each plant has 100 calories in it, and every five years the flower on it blooms. The whole flower is edible and is full of nutrients, and it helps to restore your body. It's lifespan is 7 years.

There are thousands of these plants on Venus, they grow in both cold and warm environments. Sometimes the plants die when the Ashimta parasite gets a hold of them, but luckily for the plants this rarely happens. There's one ancient volcano on Venus, but it's gone dormant 100 years ago.

The 3rd creature is the yuntis, it's the size of a bear, and is a carnivore. At times this creature can get very aggressive towards the other creatures, it preys on two different kinds of creatures.

The crabodonus and tinoota are the size of a large dog, with long distended ears. It's back legs are short and muscular it's front legs are much longer than the back legs. Both creatures feed on grasses, that only grow by the waterfall.

The water that flows down the waterfall has a high pH level; they enjoy drinking from the waterfall. The yuntis sneaks up on its prey, and attacks with great accuracy.

Oddly enough this creature won't go after its prey if it goes into the water. The yuntis is nocturnal, and sleeps for most of the day unless it's provoked. This creature have a lifespan of 8 years, once it reaches the age of 6 it struggles to walk. The 4th creature is the nectoruum, this creature has a long neck like that of a giraffe.

There's a population of 500 of these creatures on the planet, but recently the population has dwindled due to an unknown sickness that's come upon the creatures.

The yuntis won't eat a sick nectoruum, it just leaves the diseased body lay. The nectoruum has the ability to leap like a frog but can only leap short distances without having to take a rest. This creature likes to take shelter in caves, it can also hang upside down like a bat.

It likes to eat a certain kind of insect, and when it's in danger it'll bark like a dog and it'll meow at midnight.

Researchers still aren't sure how this creature can tell time. It can see in the darkest of nights, and some nights it'll take a swim in a body of water. It's life span is 10 years. Varujan's crew of astronauts reached Lorphinetta, and a few minutes later the 3 rockets landed on the planet. Followed by the rescue drone, with the robot on board. Razmik, Masis, Nare and Kolb carefully exited the spacecraft. They found their way over to one of the 3 rockets and began taking out the military equipment that they would be putting together. I don't think that we should start assembling this weapon until the winds die down.

"How long do you figure until that's going to happen?"

"40 minutes."

At this rate we're not going to get this weapon put together.

"What about letting the robot put it together?"

“That’s a very good idea, but if it makes a mistake then that's on us.”

I'm afraid that when I start putting the bolts on the equipment, they may get blown away by the wind.

Perhaps you should call Varujan or mission control, we're not going to do that. We can't rely on everyone else to make all our decisions for us.

Razmik walked over to the robot who was beginning to unload things from the second rocket. The robot quickly turned around to look at him, hello droid 1 one I hope that I didn’t interrupt you.

“Do you think it's too windy to work up here?”

“No,” Sir.

“How long would you figure it would take you to assemble the weapon?”

“Two hours if we're lucky.”

“Would you let me assist you with it?”

“I sure will.”

“Why are you looking over at Nare?”

“There's a rock monster approaching her”

The robot quickly ran over to her and pushed her out of the way. The rock monster took a swing at the robot, just barely missing him.

The robot quickly pulled out his ray gun from his side and shot the rock monster, causing it to crumble.

"Do you think anymore rock monsters are going to attack us?"

"No," I don't think so.

That rock monster attacked us because we were too close to his territory. One time I saw 22 rock monsters on one planet, but luckily at that time they weren't after me.

"What do you think they would have done to you?"

"Kill me or take me hostage."

"Do you know how rock monsters are created?"

"Yes," I do.

They're created when there's a lightning storm over a volcano that just erupted, that must be something to behold.

"How long do you figure a rock monster lives?"

"I don't know."

Chapter 4

Suddenly the robot ran over to the rocket and opened one of its compartments taking out a shovel and walked back over to the astronauts.

The robot scanned the horizon, and it's system alerted it that there would be a solar flare passing over the planet. You're acting awfully erratic Droid 1; I don't know what you're what up to.

> "Why are you digging a hole here?"
>
> "So that we can hide in it when the solar flare passes over the planet."

I doubt all of us are going to fit into that hole you dug, there's no time for us to be arguing. In 3 minutes and 45 seconds the solar flare will be passing over the planet.

Razmik brought to the attention of the other astronauts that there was going to be a solar flare passing over the planet.

Nare was frightened after hearing the news and was the first astronaut to jump into the hole, even though the robot wasn't done digging it. Masis got down into the hole next to Nare.

Then the rest of the astronauts got into the hole, along with the robot. The robot yelled out 1 minute and 5 seconds left, Razmik happened to look up from the hole at the right time and saw the solar flare lighting up the sky as it was coming towards them. He quickly put his head down and braced for impact, the other astronauts followed suit, along with the robot.

As the flare made a final approach to the planet it suddenly exploded, the explosion was so strong that it blew over the rockets. One of the rockets fell over the hole the astronauts were in, instantly causing fear to set into their minds.

Razmik thought to himself we're never going to get out of here, while Kolb was thinking about how they were going to get out of there.

Nare was disgruntled when she opened her eyes and it was pitch black, the robot covered her mouth before she could let out a scream.

Your scream would only have made the situation a lot more stressful that's the reason I did that. Don't worry everyone I'm going to get us out of here, we'd appreciate that Mr. robot.

Razmik watched as the robot placed his hands on the rocket and pushed the rocket off of them. Nare shouted out were free at last, they gave each other a hug.

Once everyone was out of the hole they began looking over the equipment to see if it was damaged in any way from the explosion.

On the second rocket there was a deep indentation probably from a space rock bouncing off of it.

Most of the paint on the rocket had melted off, from the intense temperature coming off of the solar flare.

The astronauts and the robot happened to look up and saw that there were 10 rescue crafts scanning the planet for survivors.

"Do you think they know we're here?"

"Yes," they do.

They'd only come down here to rescue us if the scanner showed that one of us was injured. Then the rescue crafts flew off into space, I'm glad that they weren't alien spacecrafts.

Razmik continued to help the robot unpack all three rockets, Nare began to read the instructions on how to put the weapon together. Kolb was taking inventory of the parts that were included with the weapon.

He was surprised to find a bag of extra bolts. Masis let out a yawn and red through the instructions with Nare.

A few minutes later all the parts to the weapon were unpacked, in an orderly fashion. A lizard looking creature came crawling over to them, and the robot scared it away.

You could have left that lizard here; it wasn't hurting anything. That lizard is very poisonous and 1 bite would kill a human, you're lucky it didn't go near your face.

It would have spit acid on your helmet melting it, then you would had died after being exposed to the element.

Then by all means you should shoot it; it's already gone so forget about it. 2 hours and 20 minutes later, the weapon was assembled.

Next came the test firing of the weapon, they loaded the weapon with it’s plasma laser formula. The weapon could hold 300 gallons of the formula, it can shoot 300,000 times before it’s supply of formula is depleted.

All the astronauts stepped back when the robot aimed the weapon and pushed in the mechanism to make the weapon fire. The weapon could also be put on auto fire, the laser beam shot out at Mach 3.

The beam flew 14,128 miles before hitting the edge of 2 frozen clouds on venus, causing both clouds to melt awakening the storm birds.

The awakened stormbirds flew over to the other frozen clouds and began pecking the clouds until they broke apart releasing the rest of the storm birds.

All 37 of the storm birds were released from the once frozen clouds, one of the birds flew off without waiting for the other ones to join it. It flew quite a ways before coming to Lorphinetta, it landed on top of one of the rockets.

The robot was the first one to see it and pointed it out to the astronauts. They never saw a bird with such blue eyes before, Nare put away all the tools that they were using to build the weapon. Kolb didn’t look away from the majestic bird, Masis touched him on the shoulder. Stop staring at that ugly bird, it's awfully sinister looking.

Suddenly the bird flew off the rocket and flew after Razmik, who was walking away from the bird. It landed on his shoulder and began pecking him with its sharp beak.

Masis saw this and came running to his aide, he tried shoving the bird off of his shoulder but it barely budged. “Get off of my friend you ugly bird he shouted, then it landed on his helmet and left out a loud screech. The bird was pecking at his helmet, he spun around hoping that the bird would fall off his helmet.

He bent over and walked forward almost into the boulder nearby, but the birds reflexes were just too quick and it jumped off his helmet and landed on the ground.

He ran away from the bird, accidentally bumping into the robot. The robot immediately stopped what he was doing and looked at him. There's a bird flying around here that won't stop attacking us.

Take me to where it was last, it was right next to the rocket over here. The bird came out of hiding and flew right for the robot who pulled out his laser shooter and shot the bird. The birds feathers turned red, and a blue protective shield appeared around the bird.

2 bolts of electricity came out of the bird, and struck the robot in the chest, knocking him over, He was able to get back up a few minutes later. After that happened the bird flew away and flew a while to get back with the other birds.

The birds could hear and feel the frequencies coming from the earth, so they began their maiden flight to earth.

Chapter 5

After quite some time the birds reached the earth's atmosphere, they were over the state of Kansas.

The birds didn't sense that there were any thunderstorms going on in that area, so they left and made their way over to Arizona. There wasn't just 1 thunderstorm going on, but there were 3, 2 miles away from the capitol.

The people just went on with their lives, and very few of them even bothered to look up. The birds went up into the clouds, and now felt right at home. Below them, there was a supermarket and a hair salon next to it.

Several women got out of their cars and walked over to the salon, where they were greeted by a smile from one of the hairdressers.

One of the women had to wait because all the chairs were filled, she took out her phone and saw that there was a text from her son. She looked closer and noticed that it was sent to her an hour ago.

Right away she became uptight and nervous about what was going on with her son. When she read the message she was immediately relieved, her son just wanted her to know that he was making soup for lunch. She messaged her husband and put her phone back in her pocket.

Sitting off to the left of her, was an elderly woman who was smiling ear to ear. She turned and looked over at the elderly woman

“Hello Ma’am, how are you doing today?”

“I'm doing just fabulous.”

I haven't had a good perm in a while, and I like to be out and about sometimes. I have to look good for my birthday tomorrow, I'll be turning 80 years old.

Happy early birthday, I hope that you enjoy your big day. Thanks so much, I'm sure that I will. The elderly woman lowered her head, I can't believe my Steve passed away a month now. She stood up and gave the elderly woman a hug, tears began running down the woman's eyes.

Not many other people are as nice to me as you’re being right now. Just the other day I took my grocery list with me, and I lost the list. I pulled into the grocery stores parking lot, and it was a very warm day, so I opened all the car doors.

After doing that I began looking over my vehicle high and low for the list, many people walked past me but didn't ask if I needed help.

That day I walked around my vehicle 4 times looking in the trunk and the back seat and the passenger seat for the list.

I couldn't believe that I was tired just after doing that, so I closed up all the doors and sat in the passenger seat and took a nap.

That's when a young man knocked on my window and asked me if I was okay. I don't remember much after that.

After quite a lengthy conversation between both women, the hairdresser called the elderly woman over to sit in the chair.

“Hello Ma’am, what would you like today?”

“I would like my usual perm please.”

“Would you also like a hair washing?”

“No,” thanks.

The young woman who was talking to the elderly woman walked out of the salon because she just couldn't wait anymore.

Many miles away from there, was an RC airplane contest going on at the small local airport. Hundreds of small remote-controlled airplanes were flying through the air, until everyone looked up and saw the storm clouds coming in. Some of the hobbyists stopped flying and packed up their stuff and left.

The stormbirds flew down from their cloud and began attacking the people walking around the grocery store parking lot.

One of the birds die bombed the man who was holding his umbrella and it’s sharp beak stuck into his arm causing the man to drop his umbrella and yell.

Blood was flowing out of his arm, just seeing it caused him to go into a tizzy. He took off his wristwatch from his right hand and tried hitting the bird with it.

It quickly got its beak unstuck from his arm and flew away. When someone saw the blood flowing out of his arm they immediately called 911.

Several minutes later an ambulance showed up, the man waved the driver down. The storm birds in the meantime continued attacking their unsuspected victims.

An off-duty police officer pulled into the parking at the grocery store. When he saw the birds flying down from the sky and attacking the people, he pulled out his trusty sidearm.

He brought the gun up and aimed and fired hitting 2 of the birds, this only stunned them for a moment, he couldn't believe that the birds survived getting shot.

Three of the birds were coming straight for him, the gunshot caused panic and people began running every which way to escape.

He placed his gun back in his holster and made a run for it, to the entrance of the grocery store. But he didn't quite make it and the birds stuck their sharp beaks straight into his back.

Once again the birds struggled but were able to get their beaks out of his back and flew off. Just the agony alone and the blood loss caused him to black out.

The ambulance driver saw where the officer had fallen and drove the ambulance over to him. The man with the deep gash in his arm was complaining and asking for more pain medication.

There's no way I'm getting out of this truck until we get to the hospital. There's birds all over the place out there, hundreds of people are going to be attacked.

The paramedic dragged the officer into the back of the ambulance and began treating him for his injuries.

Chapter 6

Both men were taken to the hospital as quickly as the driver could drive them there. All the storm birds flew out of the area and flew for a while before sensing another thunderstorm in Dallas, Texas.

There were many massive clouds in the sky, some lightning bolts came out of the clouds and struck the road below.

There were many cars driving down the street, some of the drivers had their moon roofs open, to take in some fresh air.

2 stormbirds flew down from the clouds and followed the cars going down the road. The bird sped up and flew down through the sunroof of one of the cars, the driver of the car was texting while driving. The birds were walking around on the back seat exploring, after that they flew up and landed on the passenger seat. The man happened to look over and saw the birds.

He dropped his phone and was so shocked that he crashed into the car in front of him. The birds landed on the steering wheel; the man was trying desperately to get his seat belt off but it was jammed.

It was already too late for him, both birds landed on him and began pecking his throat, causing him to bleed to death.

Somehow the birds were able to figure out the way that they came in and flew out of the car and back up into the clouds.

There were 3 Apache helicopters, on their way to the military base. They were flying just below the clouds and didn't know how close they were to danger.

One of the helicopters sped up when a lightning bolt narrowly struck it. The sound of the helicopters angered the birds, so they flew out of the cloud and toward the helicopters.

The pilots saw the birds and quickly veered away from them. The birds could no longer keep up with them, they lost interest and went back up into the clouds.

An hour later the thunderstorms were over and the sky cleared up. The birds were no longer content, they flew away looking for more thunderstorms somewhere else.

They flew over Florida and surprisingly, there were no storms there. Sometime later the birds went to South Carolina, there were 3 thunderstorms going on at the same time.

They came to an area where there was a new development being built, one of the many builders carried several pieces of wood over to the home that he was working on.

While another builder was putting up the walls, with help from another builder. Nearby the stormbirds landed in two 2 trees, they kept their eyes on the builders every move. After a while the builders took a break and sat down to eat they're sandwiches, chips and drink their bottled water.

You know Mac, I think that I'm going to become a vegetarian. That was awfully random, I brought it up because my wife and I have been discussing it.

Meat is skyrocketing in price, and my wife told me to lose some weight. I don't think you need to lose any weight, just by looking at you, I feel the same way you do about it.

I'm 198 pounds, she wants me to come down to 180 pounds. On the radio the weather forecaster said that there's a chance there's going to be a hailstorm in this area.

I rarely believe anything that they say these days, the skies cloudy, but it doesn't mean that it's going to rain if they say it will.

"How's your truck running these days?"

"It's been running terribly."

The other day it's transmission went on me leaving me on the side the road, luckily I was able to reach my buddy on his phone and he came down to help me. A week after getting it fixed the clutch went on me, you just have no luck with trucks.

"How old is that truck?"

"It's a 2017 Ford Pickup truck."

You should just get rid of that thing and get a 2022, but the brand-new trucks are awfully expensive.

The one man pointed to 2 large trees off to the right side of them. I've never seen such odd-looking birds; don't take a picture of them you might spook them.

You can keep bird watching and I'm going to get back to work. Suddenly the birds flew out of the tree towards them, we need to find cover from them.

There probably just typical crows, and they'll just leave us all alone. The birds went after the men, pecking them and stabbing them with their sharp beaks.

The man who survived the attacks immediately jumped in their trucks and took off, 2 out of the 5 builders were lying on the ground in agony.

Minutes later the birds finished them off by stabbing them to death. The birds quickly flew away from the scene, they enjoyed the thunderstorms until they were over.

After that they went on another journey to find more storms, quite some time later they ended up in New York city. Where there were some thunderstorms going on.

They could see there reflections in the tall glass buildings, every one of the birds forcefully slammed into one of the windows of a tall building.

When the people inside saw the birds, they took cover under their desks, the screams from the people seemed to only anger the birds.

The birds landed on the floor, and we're walking around looking for the people. When one of the office phones went off, the birds immediately went after it, destroying it with their sharp talons.

After doing that, they went back to hunting the people. One of the people brought out a pepper sprayer out of their pocket, to be ready for a bird attack.

Eventually the birds found the people and began attacking them, the people kicked the birds in efforts to stop them.

Someone threw an open bottle of white out at the birds, in hopes of blinding them, but it did nothing to stop the birds.

One woman stood up and made it run for it, to the bathroom so she could hide in there from the birds. One of the birds flew into her back, stabbing her in the shoulder.

She cried out and quickly got into the bathroom, closing the door behind her. A few minutes later everyone else was murdered by the birds, except for the woman who was hiding in the bathroom.

The woman stayed in the bathroom for another 20 minutes, when she opened the door she was relieved to see that the birds were gone.

The birds broke into 2 more buildings and attacked several more people, before resting on top of a building.

On the top of a building close to them was the security man, he looked through the riflescope at the birds and fired at several of them hitting and killing 2 of them.

Suddenly both birds that were hit came back to life, the birds came after the man mercilessly. After just a few minutes the man laid there dead from his many injuries all over his body.

After that the birds were feeling tired and decided to fly to a woodland area and land in 2 trees and rest there for a while. The very next day, the birds left earth and returned to Venus.

The elite team of astronauts and the robot returned to earth, Varujan came back to the United States from vacation, where his fiancé was waiting for him.

The Police officers in Spain worked for another month then went on vacation. The bulls were all captured by the cowboys in town and returned to the arenas.

www.ingramcontent.com/pod-product-compliance
Lightning Source LLC
LaVergne TN
LVHW020531160826
845677LV00015B/3998
* 9 7 9 8 3 6 7 7 9 8 9 5 1 *